COYUNNA

Believe in yourself

THE BUGGUZZ
Let There Be Light

CREATED BY: ANGI MARI YANGAS
ILLUSTRATED BY: CLAUDIA LA BIANCA

This book is dedicated to my Uncle Bruno who taught me the three C's many years ago.
Thanks Uncle Bru...I love you.

And a special thanks to Lee Graves

For further information,
please contact: binxbooks@gmail.com

Book design by Angi Mari Yangas and Claudia La Bianca

Printed in the United States

Bugguzz: Let There Be Light
Angi Mari Yangas
1. Title 2. Author 3. Children's Book

Library of Congress Control Number: 2007909282
ISBN 10: 0-9801796-0-2
ISBN 13: 978-0-9801796-0-6

Welcome to fabulous Los Nostriles, the city of boogers.
The streets are paved in gold and the skyscrapers are made
of only the finest boogers in your nose. HMMM… maybe
that's where the saying came from, "What are you diggin' for- Gold?"
Well, it's no longer Saturday here in Los Nostriles, it's Saturnight and the
city is bumpin'. Everyone's ready to go out and have a super sligitty slammin',
totally rockin' good time!

The Bugguzz are hangin' out in their penthouse watching cartoons and preparing for their night out, when out of nowhere- BOOM DZIT! It's dark. As Ozz cruised around their crib looking for the circuit breaker, Beboop peered out the window and realized... UHH-OHH! It's not just the penthouse that's dark, it's the entire city! All of Los Nostriles is blacked out!

"I'm scared!" Keybe cried out to his posse. "Where do we go? What do we do? Most importantly, how are we going to find the flashlight so we can get where we're suppose to go and do what we're suppose do? AHHHHH!" Keybe screamed.

"Keybe, slow down!" Ahhpoom advised him. "Breathe in. Breathe out. Relax. Don't panic, we know what to do in situations like this." Ahhpoom reminded him. "First of all, you have to remember the three C's whenever you find yourself in any kind of trouble: Cool, Calm, and Collected. Next, you go to the designated area in the house that we all agreed on. From there, you go and get the flashlight in the special spot that we all picked out together. It's next to the telephone in the TV room, which IS the designated area, in case you forgot. Now, go get the flashlight so you aren't scared anymore." Ahhpoom instructed him.

"Oh Ahhpoom, you always now exactly what to say to make everything all better!" Keybe professed as he batted his eyelashes at her in total admiration. "Let's go girl!" He giggled as he grabbed her hand and made her go with him to get the flashlight.

Ahhpoom smiled and went with Keybe so he wouldn't be scared.

4

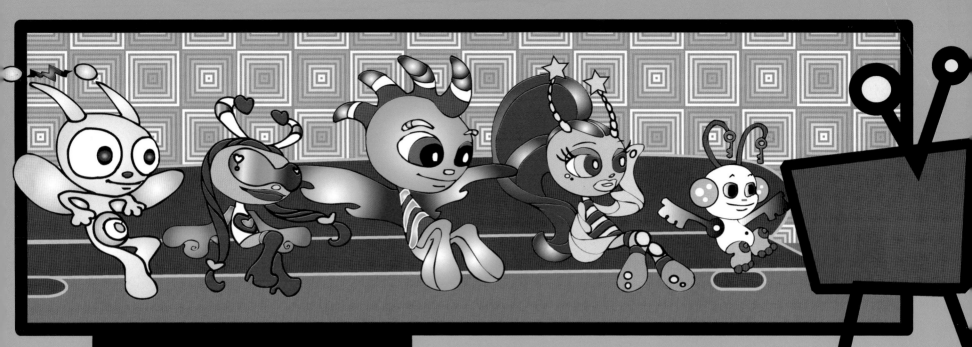

5

"Come on!" Beboop shouted somewhat annoyed. "There's no time to waste." He urged his posse to get going. "We need to find the Stuff and figure out how they blacked out all of Los Nostriles."

"You're right, Beboop," Ozz interjected, "but before we go, you have to put your belly to use. There's no way we'll be able to save Los Nostriles if we can't see where we're going!" Ozz told him. "It's your time to shine, Beboop!"

Beboop agreed with total excitement. It's not often that he gets to light up his belly. In case you don't know, his belly shoots out a thirty-three million-watt searchlight that targets the Stuff within a three-mile radius. (The light is only visible to the Bugguzz though, so the Stuff never know when they've been detected.)

Beboop proudly lit up his belly and his posse cheered and squinted, they were almost blinded by the light!

"There's no stopping us now!" The Bugguzz sang. "We're on the move!"

They were off, ready to save Los Nostriles, on the most important night of the week, Saturnight.

Kalypsi and Ahhpoom jumped in the Vita-C SUV and gave it some juice. VAVAVAVOOM! They zoomed off the rooftop with Ozz, Keybe and Beboop quick to follow and comment on the girls.

"Why do they get to drive?" Keybe complained to the guys as he tried to keep up with them.

"Shouldn't I have some kind of car seat in the Vita-C SUV to make sure I'm safe? I mean, seriously, I'm a baby!" Keybe whined.

"Stop feeling sorry for yourself cry baby, and try to keep up with us." Beboop suggested to Keybe whose little wings couldn't flap any faster.

"Okay guys, this should be fun, ready?" Ozz asked them as he pulled out a megaphone from behind him. "Everyone knows that girls are the worst drivers!" He shouted as loud as he possibly could into the megaphone.

EEERRRRTTTT! Slamming on the brakes and staring in the rearview mirror while she applied her lipstick, not to mention her mascara, and listening to her daily horoscope on her cell phone, Kalypsi replied. "Forty-three percent of all accidents are caused by the driver getting distracted so if you'd be so kind and zip-it, Ozz, then I can continue driving safely! Thank you very much." Kalypsi fumed with attitude.

"HA-HA-HA, we're outtie!" The girls laughed as they burned rubber through Los Nostriles leaving the guys standing there shocked, in a cloud of dust.

"They can't be that dumb." Ozz mumbled as he coughed up some dust.

"Well, they are both really pretty. You can't have everything." Beboop grumbled. "Look at me, I'm a genius with a target on my belly!" That makes me the living proof!"

The guys looked at each other in agreement.

Ozz, Keybe and Beboop took off, trying to catch up with the girls, flying through the city of boogers in search of the power outage. Out of nowhere, they started smelling the most foul smell ever. It was stinking up the entire city! It smelled like the worst smelling sweaty foot you've ever smelled, times one hundred billion, combined with twenty-three overflowing Port-a-Potties, on a steamy hot and humid, eighty degree day! YOWZA!

"I can't breathe!" Beboop gasped.

"This can't be good for my complexion!" Kalypsi shouted. "Citrusonium vapor on!"

The Vita-C SUV shot out the Citrusonium vapor, which turns any poo-poo ca-ca smell into the most deliciously fresh-n-fruity, clean, citrus scent. Within a few seconds, the Bugguzz could breathe again so they continued on, truckin' through Los Nostriles with big smiles on their faces in search of the Stuff.

"There's no power like citrus power." Beboop cheered happily along with the rest of the Bugguzz.

The cheering quickly came to a stop when…

"HUMMMM, what's that ahead of us?" Ozz questioned his posse as they flew into South Central.

All together at the same time the Bugguzz screamed, "It's the Stuff: Mumpsolumpso, Flukey Pukey, Bakteriyuck and Blotina Crampina! Where's Germsly Chunk-Chunk, though," the Bugguzz wondered, "and why are the Stuff here in South Central?"

Before they had a spare second to figure out the answers to their questions…

"Oh no, they've spotted us!" Ozz shouted. "Everyone charge up!" All the Bugguzz pushed their Vita-C buttons on their bellies and their very own squirt bottle filled with the super special succulent, California neon orange, Vita-C O J, superpowered, saucy, Citrusonium concoction appeared, and they all slammed it! Now, they're super charged and ready to kick some Stuff! Before they can start the kickin', they have to figure out the answers to their questions.

The Bugguzz were flying above the Stuff trying to spot Germsly Chunk-Chunk and figure out why the Stuff are in South Central when…

"Of course," Beboop sighed as he hit himself in the head, "it's SO obvious! UHH-DUH! We completely overlooked the fact that The Los Nostriles Water and Power Plant is here in South Central." Beboop elaborated. "I have no doubt that somehow the Stuff must have stopped the juicer, which would explain why all of Los Nostriles is blacked out."

"That's it, Beboop, for sure!" Ahhpoom agreed. "Without the juicer squeezing fresh O J into the juice lines, there's no energy to be processed and transferred through the high tension wires to create electricity." Ahhpoom energetically added.

"Let's get em'," the Bugguzz yelled, "and get em' good!"

They flew straight towards the Stuff ready for an all out street brawl. Since Keybe has the keys to the city, his wings, he flew straight into the water and power plant building to check the juicer so he could try to unlock the problem. Within a few seconds, the Bugguzz and the Stuff were ready to face off.

Ozz yelled in his announcer voice, "Let's get ready to rumble!"

The Bugguzz and the Stuff charged at one another.

Blotina Crampina snarled at the Bugguzz, "Nobody betta come near me, or I'll sit on top of 'em and squish the life right outta vum, ya hear?"

Before she even knew what hit her, Ahhpoom flew over Blotina Crampina and dropped a Vita-C bomb on top of her pointy-head. BA-BA-BA-BOOM! Blotina Crampina exploded and water drenched the area like a tidal wave.

"That's some serious water retention!" Ahhpoom giggled. "Next time, you better remember not to mess with me. I'm Ahhpoom Atomic!" She continued on giggling.

The rest of The Stuff began drowning in the water, but the Bugguzz weren't going to let them off that easy. Ozz grabbed Bacteriyuck and gave him a Vita-C punch that knocked him right out of Los Nostriles. Green bacteria splattered through out the city. No need to worry because Beboop was there with the industrial-sized, super suctioning, supped-up, Vita-C vacuum to get rid of all the bacteria that spread through out the beautiful city of boogers.

In the mean time, Kalypsi took care of Flukey Pukey, and Ozz attacked Mumpsolumpso; all while Keybe finally figured out what was wrong with the juicer. Somehow, there were thousands of onions clogging it! The only thing Keybe could do was unclog all the onions so the electricity would start up again. When out of no where, Germsly Chunk-Chunk jumped out from behind the juicer and grabbed lil' Keybe.

"AAAHHHHHHH," Keybe screamed with a quiver in his voice, "somebody, anybody, PLLEEAASSSEE, help me!" Keybe cried. "It's Germsly Chunk-Chunk, and he's going to-" GULP!

"Baby Bugguzz don't taste that bad," Germsly Chunk-Chunk grunted, "a little salty, kind of like chicken." He chuckled with some satisfaction in his voice as he began clogging the juicer even more. "Now, all I need is some fresh sewer water to wash down my delicious dinner, HA-HA-HA!" He cackled.

Ozz, Beboop, Kalypsi and Ahhpoom were finished beating up the Stuff, when for some reason, they began to feel like something was wrong. They were in flight towards the juicer when they all looked at each other at the same time and asked, "Where's Keybe been, and why is that horrendously repulsive smell getting even stronger?"

Confused why the power was still not on and concerned about Keybe, the Bugguzz continued on squeamishly in search of some answers. Then far off in the distance they heard something. They remembered to stay Cool, Calm, and Collected as they followed the noise. They realized the smell was getting stronger, too. That could only mean one thing- Germsly Chunk-Chunk! The Bugguzz flew faster trying to find him. When they spotted him, they snuck up and began spying. They couldn't believe their ears!

"I'm finally going to conquer Los Nostriles." Germsly Chunk-Chunk hissed to himself. "Burp, UGH, that baby Bugguzz is giving me gas!" He roared, as he stood burping and tooting the melody of Twinkle Twinkle Little Star, on top of the mountain of onions he was throwing into the California grown oranges ONLY juicer.

"Not if we have anything to do with it!" The Bugguzz yelled as they flew towards him and the juicer. "Get him!"

18

By then, the Citrusonium vapor had worn out and the Bugguzz could barely breathe because of Germsly Chunk-Chunks nasty halitosis breath. The posse flew towards him each with one hand clenched in a fist and the other one holding their nose. Ahhpoom found a piece of super, sticky, icky, chewy, gooey, acid, orange, bionic, blowing bubble gum and began to blow a giant bubble. She blew and blew and blew, and the bubble got bigger and bigger and bigger until finally-
BA-BA-BA-BOOM!

"Look!" Kalypsi said gleefully. "Orange acid is falling all over Germsly Chunk-Chunk and his mountain of onions!"

"That's because of me, and you better not forget it!" Ahhpoom shouted at Germsly Chunk-Chunk. I'm Ahhpoom Acidic! Put that in your sewer water and drink it!" She giggled uncontrollably.

"This isn't the last of me you microscopic imbeciles! AHHHHH, the acid, I'm melting, and my beautiful onions are rotting into mush! This can't be happening to me!" Germsly Chunk-Chunk shrieked in distress.

"Oh, but it is, you smelly, dirty, little, disgusting chunk of ca-ca." The Bugguzz shouted.

BA-BA-BA-BA-BOOM

21

"Hey look, it's Keybe!" Beboop gasped.

Keybe flew up out of Germsly Chunk-Chunks melting body with a dazed look on his face, and his fingers squeezing his nose. The top of his head looked like it was smoking, and it was! It was on fire! Germsly Chunk-Chunks stomach must have started digesting Keybe!

"Somebody help him!" Beboop screamed.

"Hurry, Keybe, pull my finger!" Kalypsi instructed him. Oh no, wait, OOPS! I mean stop, drop and roll!"

Keybe followed Kalipsi's instructions perfectly. First, some gas was passed, and then the fire was out!

"You have no idea how happy I am to see my posse!" Keybe marveled, almost in tears. "I was wondering, what the heck was taking you guys so long? It doesn't matter, now that I'm still alive. I love you guys. I really, really love you guys!" Keybe gushed, as he smiled at his posse.

The Bugguzz smiled back, plugged their noses and gave Keybe a big huge bug hug. They were so thankful that he was okay, and Los Nostriles was okay, too, at least for today.

Keybe unlocked the juicer and the Bugguzz began the clean up. The acid got rid of pretty much all of the onions, so cleaning up wasn't too big of a hassle. When the Bugguzz were finished they shouted for all of Los Nostriles to hear- "Let there be light!"

The city lit up, and the people cheered, "HIP-HIP-HORRAY! YIPEEEEEE! YA-HIBBITTY-WHOO!"

All the Los Nostrilans danced around the streets celebrating. The lights were back on and Saturnight was saved!

Even though the hardest part of the night was over, the Bugguzz still had some more work to do. First, they decided that they needed to invent an invisible force field sphere for Keybe, just in case he ever gets eaten alive again. Next, they had to prepare the hot tub…

"Help me! Please help me!" Keybe screamed as the Bugguzz stood over him with their fingers still plugging their noses, scrubbing and dunking and dunking and scrubbing him in the strongest, Citrusonium, extra pulp added, ultra, mega, disinfecting, fresh squeezed, California grown, sunshine filled, orange juice bubble bath.

"Sorry Keybe, it's the only way to get Germsly Chunk-Chunks putrid smell off of you." The Bugguzz comforted him as they continued dunking and scrubbing and scrubbing and dunking him.

Keybe had smelled SO bad, that he paint on the penthouse walls was peeling off! Once the Bugguzz were able to unplug their noses and not gag, they knew their job was almost done.

"I can breathe without smelling poopy!" Keybe blubbered with happiness as he grabbed his invisible force field sphere and rolled around the penthouse floor knocking everything over!

The Bugguzz were cracking up watching Keybe destroy the penthouse. By the time they could grab him, it looked like a tornado had hit!

"Our work will never be done." The Bugguzz joked as they sat back, kicked up their feet and sipped on kiddie cocktails with extra cherries while they watched Keybe clean up the disaster he just made…all by his lil' lonesome self! AWWWWW!

These microscopic beings, will never stop being, Los Nostriles dwelling, Stuff destroying, defenders to human beings. They love their Vita-C and protecting you and me. There isn't much they ask, just these few simple tasks: Get plenty of sleep, drink your O J everyday, to keep you strong and healthy, repeat what I say: Shake it, don't fake it, blow it, don't break it, tell a lie and it'll grow, the Bugguzz live inside your nose. So be safe, and be careful, in all that you do. Especially when you feel like... AHH, AHH, AHH-CHOO!

The moral of the story kids is to remember the three C's: Cool, Calm, and Collected whenever you find yourself in any kind of trouble. You should always be prepared for situations like this. Have a designated area in your house that you go to in case there's ever an emergency. Always know where you keep your flashlight so you don't have to search around in the dark for it. Most importantly, don't be worried because the lights always go back on, just give it a little time. While you're waiting, have as much fun as you possibly can by, telling stories, singing songs and playing games (obviously ones that don't require too much light!). Like always, remember to keep drinking your orange juice because it's the only way you can fight off the Stuff that makes you sick, and one last thing, keep your finger out of your nose, DO NOT PICK!

THE BUGGUZZ SONG

THHHHHHEEEEEEEY...
LIVE IN LOS NOSTRILES AND THAT'S IN YOUR NOSE!
THEY'RE MICROSCOPIC BEINGS THAT NO ONES EVER KNOWN.
THEY'RE THE BUGGUZZ,

B-U-G-G-U-Z-Z

AND WHAT I'M 'BOUT TO TELL YOU WILL MAKE HISTORY!
THEY FLY UP YOUR HOLE AND YOU NEVER EVEN KNOW!
ONCE YOU MEET 'EM YOU'LL SAY GIMMIE SOME MO'!
THEY FIGHT ALL THE STUFF THAT MAKES US SICK,
SO KEEP YOUR FINGER OUT OF YOUR NOSE,

DO NOT PICK!